THE BOX
AND MY TROUBLE
GETTING IT

THE BOX
AND MY TROUBLE
GETTING IT

BRUCE B. TRYON

authorHOUSE®

AuthorHouse™
1663 Liberty Drive
Bloomington, IN 47403
www.authorhouse.com
Phone: 1 (800) 839-8640

Published by AuthorHouse 03/29/2018

ISBN: 978-1-5462-3518-7 (sc)
ISBN: 978-1-5462-3517-0 (hc)
ISBN: 978-1-5462-3516-3 (e)

Library of Congress Control Number: 2018903769

Print information available on the last page.

Chapter 1

HOSPITAL LANDING PAD

WE HAD BARELY TOUCHED DOWN at the hospital landing pad when Captain Milroy pushed open the hatch door and started running. I caught a glimpse of him running from the ship for the hospital door when he almost stumbled - he managed to recover and continued to run for the door. The hospital's sliding doors didn't open fast enough so he crashed into them and kept on going.

Several minutes later we caught up with him in the hallway, looking dazed as someone hurried through a set of sliding doors with the box of medical supplies under his arm.

We stood for a few minutes before Kilo turned to the captain and, said, "Okay, now what?"

The Captain looked around at all of us and said, "Come on. Let's go to my brother's place. He said he would meet us there later with news."

Walking back to the space ship I had a small chance to look around at this planet. It was green and brown, with patches of other colors. I could hear birds, insects and something else making noise in the woods. When we were coming down from space I was not able to see the planet because I had been confined to my quarters since the outpost. When we landed I was told by Kilo and Kilos that I was not allowed to be left alone on the space ship until I was either convicted or cleared of what had happened on the outpost. Since they did not want to stay on board, and since I had already been partially cleared of the initial charges, they decided to take me with them to the hospital.

While Kilo and Kilos escorted me to the hospital, I was more interested in what was in that box and if we had been in time. After all, that would also have an impact on my trial. Although I am considered to be tall, walking between these two made me feel like a short story between two bookends.

Curious, I asked the Captain, "Who was that man who disappeared behind the doors?"

"Oh! That's my brother and Fitzroy's father, Gilroy."

"But aren't Kilo, the First officer, and Kilos, the Navigational officer, related to you and Gilroy, too?

"Yes, Kilo and Kilos are my sons and Fitzroy is Gilroy's son."

Well, that was a surprise to me. I had only signed on with this shipping company for a month before the incident. There was no indication that it was a family run operation although some of the crew was more familiar to each other. I was only just beginning to figure out the relationships between the different crewmembers. I still think it wouldn't have made any difference to me—I was a long way from home and needed to earn credit to head home. My name is Joneb and I started out in a space colony on Deneb, the other side of the Milky Way.

Space travel was a way to escape from the everyday humdrum existence on my planet, even if I missed my family, particularly my Mom and my older brother. However, that's another story. I have had a variety of adventures some more exciting than others. My last one was particularly harrowing and I was rather glad to sign on to an interplanetary freighting company that seemed to be fairly routine in its operation, with no surprises, or so I thought.

When I had signed on to the Star Struck, the Captain had mentioned that the crew was close knit and I might have problems fitting in. I was used to being the odd man out since I had often changed jobs I started working on space ships. Captain Milroy thought it through; fortunately, my former Captain from the space ship, Wanderlust, had given me a good recommendation.

"Joneb, I think I will hire you for a six-month contract with the option of a 2-year contract after that. How does that sound to you?"

"Well, that sounds great sir! I certainly look forward to serving with you. You won't regret it."

"I certainly hope not. Now, wind up your affairs

and report back here by curfew tonight. I want to leave by first sunrise."

"Yes, Sir!" I strode down the airlock feeling on top of the universe. Finally, a new start, another chance to earn some space credits. I might even be able to start working my way homeward.

After I joined the Star Struck it took the better part of a month to settle in. I had just started feeling comfortable with the crew. Jacson, Upjohn, David and I shared quarters, 4 small bunks in a room with 4 chairs and a table, typical quarters for a small freighter. Upjohn was one of the captain's sons, but David, Jacson and I were the non-family members. David was from the same planet but Jacson hailed from the next planetary system. Fitzroy, Mikeroy and Rojas were brothers and sister. Their father was the Captain's brother, Gilroy. Jonroy, the other female officer was the captain's daughter. Fitzroy, Rojas, Mikeroy and Jonroy also shared quarters. That left Kilos, (also the Captain's son) Roy (another son of Milroy), and Raymond (also from the same planet) for the 3rd crew room. Of course, the captain, Milroy and the first officer, Kilo had their own quarters. Jonroy and Rojas were the only female members of the crew. Although I knew it was crazy, I was beginning to fall in love with Rojas. Who was I kidding I was completely lost—I never knew I could feel this way about anyone. Well, enough about me for now. I was still trying to figure out what had happened and why as we headed for the Star Struck.

The captain walked out of the hospital a bit more slowly. We went back to the spaceport and boarded the Star Struck.

"Ah! Captain?"

"Yes, Joneb."

"Where is your brother's house? Are we going to be able to land the ship there?"

"No. We have to take the shuttle to his house.

On the shuttle, Fitzroy asked. "Captain did you get my father's key card for the door?"

"No. Don't you have yours?"

"No."

"Why not?"

"When I moved out, I gave it back to him. What about the rest of you?", he asked, looking at his brothers and sister.

From the sheepish looks, no one had the necessary key card.

"Oops! I guess we're just going to have to wait outside for him."

We walked to the house in almost total silence. We reached the house, which only took a few minutes.

Both men stopped in front of the door they looked accusingly at one another. As I looked around everyone looked upset at either the Captain or maybe Fitzroy. Then all of a sudden, the Captain started to laugh. First one then another began to laugh or smile as tensions relaxed. As I looked at Rojas, who is the Captain's niece as well as the communication officer, she softened and gave me a soft smile which warmed me and made me blush, I think because I felt hot which was either from that look or the heat or from the hard look I got from the Captain.

I guessed it could be several hours before the captain's brother, Gilroy came home from the hospital but there was no way to tell. I looked around for a chair but all I saw were some three--legged stools.

They had some sort of fabric stretched between the legs. I stood there and watched while one of the crew started to sit down. Then the stool moved. I blinked and looked again at the stool and it moved up to meet the crewmember. It spread out to fit the size of that person. The stool had greenish brown legs with a brownish type of fabric stretched between the legs. We call them "stoolies", the Captain said. "Don't ask. The scientists still haven't figured them out. But they come in handy for sitting.

I turned around and leaned on the railing of the porch. I looked out on a brook coming out from under the house. There were tall trees on both sides of the brook. Some were brown with green leaves while other trees were reddish with purple tinged leaves.

The brook flowed down the hill. With the silence on the porch I could hear the waterfall and the water seemed to go on to the ocean or was it a lake-from this distance I could not really tell.

I stood and stared at the water flowing from under the house tuning out the argument that started up about the box and me.

I watched birds fly around and heard some insects fly around as well. I was watching a bug of some sort crawl along a leaf of a nearby plant.

I am not sure how long I watched the bug move over the leaves and flowers before I noticed a flower that had fringes on the edges of the petals. The bug got stuck on the flower but before I could see what happened next someone touched me and I jumped. I looked around and to my surprise it was Rojas.

"Ah! Hi Rojas." I said.

"Is that all you can say, Hi."

"Ah! No, but I thought we were trying to keep our friendship quiet?" as she stood there the evening sunlight touched her skin. Then I looked into her eyes and lost any and all thoughts of my problems. Those eyes, those beautiful eyes, blue with a trace of green and the iris looks red or orange but with the suns setting it changed the color of her eyes a bit. Her hair was red and gold in the sun, making it hard to think of anything else, except how beautiful she was.

"We are but it looked like you needed some help staying focused on this world and me and not so much on the trial."

"But how, your Uncle has all but convicted me. I know he reinstated me, but it all hangs on the reports from the outpost."

"Things are not always what they seem," Rojas reassured me.

Gilroy arrived and looked around at everyone sitting outside on the porch.

Milroy noticed he had arrived and asked, "How's Dad?"

Gilroy turned and answered. "Father's doing fine now. It was a close call. He is resting quietly."

He looked at us. "Why are you all standing around out here?"

"We don't have a key card," said Milroy.

Gilroy laughed. "Since Fitzroy moved out, I've left the door unlocked. Just in case you or the world were giving him a rough time, he could come home anytime he wanted. I told him I would leave the door unlocked just for that reason."

Both Fitzroy and the Captain were a little red in the face.

Fitzroy turned and said. "Sorry Captain. I forgot."

We followed Gilroy into his house. He sat down and asked "by the way, what took you so long to bring me that box of vaccine? We almost lost Dad."

Milroy looked even redder in the face. "Don't ask me. Ask him. It's all his fault."

"Who?"

"Joneb." He said, as he pointed at me.

Gilroy looked at me and asked. "Okay Joneb. What happened? Why did it take you so long to get that box to me?"

"It wasn't on purpose, it just happened. All I did was hunt all around the station trying to find that box. I nearly got myself killed in the process. The captain sent me after it." I said defensively.

"So brother, why did you send him after it?" inquired Gilroy.

"I was really trying to keep him out of trouble." said Milroy wryly.

"It didn't work did it?" Gilroy laughed.

"No, it didn't." The captain shrugged, "Joneb, you'd better tell him why it took you so long to get that box."

"It's a long story." I said reluctantly.

"Fine. I want to hear all of it and with you being captain, Milroy, it should be very interesting."

"Gilroy, it *is* a long story." Milroy remarked. "Are you sure you want to hear the whole story?"

"Yes, with all the details."

"Okay, Joneb tell him."

"It all started a little over 12 hours ago..."

"I had just reported to duty. I said Hi to Rojas. She responded with a 'Hi', back. Then I asked Kilo if there was anything I needed to know, he just grunted as we passed each other. I was coming on duty and he was going off. I knew he didn't like being kept waiting so I was actually a little early. He just liked doing that to aggravate me.

He spoke abruptly over his shoulder as he left the bridge. 'Rojas will fill you in.'"

"Okay, but... before I could say another word he was gone. I turned to Rojas. What did I do?"

"Nothing. He's been like that for about an hour or so. I think he knows something is wrong and he is a bit upset."

"Rojas, why did we change course? Aren't

we supposed to be at Moon Base Alphet in the Dragoon star cluster by now?"

"'Yes, Joneb." she replied. "We were but we received a private transmission for the Captain a few hours ago from Argyle. He took it in his ready room. When he came out he walked over to Kilo and whispered to him. Then Kilo, the First Officer went over to Kilos, the navigational officer, and spoke to him. Then we changed direction. After that, the captain left the bridge,' Rojas said."

A few minutes later the captain walked on the bridge. The crew went silent. 'I want the bridge crew and the junior navigational officer to come to the mess hall in twenty minutes.' he said looking directly at me.

We walked down to the mess hall. As we entered I slipped into a seat in the back. "As you are aware, we have made a course change." the captain said. "We're going to pick up a box from a remote outpost in the Danube solar system."

He yelled. "Joneb."

"Yes, Sir!" I replied.

"I have a job for you. I need you to pick up that box for me," said the captain.

Sensing by the tone of his voice that there was something wrong, I asked, "What's wrong? What am I picking up?"

"You don't need to know. Just get it or don't come back. Because if you do return without it you'll be floating home!" he snapped.

He turned to Jacson (supply officer) and said, "You should pick up a few other supplies while we are there. We can't afford to spend too much time at the outpost."

Several hours later we docked at the Durban outpost in the Danube solar system. The captain stopped me and shoved an invoice in my hand. "Joneb, Go to the general cargo office. They'll be able to tell you where to get this. Please hurry." He said as he pushed me out the hatch.

"Why?"

"Don't ask, just go."

"Stop, why did you send him instead of one of the family to retrieve the box?" Asked Gilroy.

"If I had sent one of the family, they might not have made it." Said Milroy.

"What do you mean they might not have made it?" I asked.

"We have a slight family problem. So, I sent you instead of one of the family."

"You mean I was expendable?"

"No, you were an unknown crew member and I was hoping that you could get the box and bring it back to me without causing too much suspicion. But maybe I might have been mistaken."

"Oh, it sure seemed like they wanted to kill me or delay my departure."

"There was only a possibility of that."

"But the invoice had the name of the ship and the captain on it."

"Enough of this Joneb, just finish the story", said Gilroy.

Okay…I looked down at the flimsy plastic

and read the description of the box. As close as I could make out it was 12" square with silver bands around it as well as silver handles on both ends. There was also a Red Cross symbol on the top of the box. I also saw some more description but then had to walk quickly to catch up with the rest of the landing party, while looking around for the general cargo office.

I caught up with the landing party just inside the outpost. The general cargo office was in the opposite direction."

"And who was in this landing party?" Asked Gilroy.

"There was Fitzroy, your son, Jacson, the supply officer, Rojas, communication officer, Kilos, the Navigational officer and Upjon, the medical member of the crew.

"And where were you my dear brother?" Gilroy asked questionably.

"I was on the bridge with Kilo waiting for Joneb to get back with the vaccine."

"May I continue?"

"Yes, please."

"I saw Fitzroy ahead of me. So, I tapped him on the shoulder. I told him I had found the cargo office but it was in the opposite direction and I would meet him back at the ship. Then I asked what he was getting? But he wouldn't tell me."

Chapter 2

THE DURBAN OUTPOST

"**A**s I walked to the General cargo office I looked at the invoice. A box of vaccine – that usually means an epidemic."

"I went in and waited in line. I stood there in a daze not really thinking about much. So, I didn't hear the word 'Next' when it was called out. I did move forward but only after an alien standing behind me growled 'Move'. I really wasn't listening to that alien either. When she pushed me in the direction of the window I got the message."

I put my hands up and spoke, "alright, I'm moving, you don't have to push." As I approached the window, I started to give the invoice to the alien at the steel meshed window. I stopped, staring at what IT was wearing and had a small laugh. I had heard of this species but never encountered one face to face. It looked like a suit of armor, that IT had been poured into. With every movement the suit made a creaking sound. It sounded just like a suit of armor which was going to pop a rivet or two, then fall off. When I did look up at IT, I noticed that IT was waiting for something. I looked curiously at IT. IT pointed at my hand. When I looked down I noticed that I was still holding the invoice. I gave the invoice to IT." (Although I considered myself fairly well traveled, I had not seen that many alien—or rather non-human species. This had to be one of the more bizarre types—I believe IT was a Dillow from the Delta Quadrant.)

"IT looked at me for a moment then IT looked down at the invoice and said in a muffled tone. 'Go to window number fifteen, it is the blue one.' As IT handed back the invoice, IT pointed to the left."

"Taking the invoice, I headed down the badly lit hallway. The only illumination was over the doors; it was just enough to see the numbers. I found the blue window, which was actually number, seventeen. So, I went inside and waited in line again. A sign flashed, "Next." I moved to the window."

"A tentacle came out from a hole in the wall and I jumped back a little. I carefully put the invoice on a couple of the suction cups. After a few minutes the tentacle came out with the invoice. (This was an Octopod, from one of the water planets. They used a translation box to communicate.) Then a mechanical voice with a female tone said, "Go to the hallway, turn right. Proceed down that hallway until you get to the cargo receiving office. It is the green door after the third bulkhead marked CRO-13 Q."

"Out in the hallway again, I finally arrived at the cargo receiving office. I handed George (his name was on his uniform) the invoice (I was sort of grateful that he was human.) He looked at the invoice. Then he pointed behind me and said, 'To get to the cargo bay, you go back to the hall. Turn right; walk down the corridor until you see bulkhead number 43. Open that bulkhead; proceed to bulkhead number A-13. Do not open that one but turn left or was that right?? No, it's a left turn. Proceed down the corridor to bulkhead number Q-3345. Oh, yeah!! You'll need this to get into the cargo bay.' He handed me a metal card and the invoice."

"Thank you."

He paused, and then continued. "You will find that box up against the wall about half way down on the right side. In section 23 no 24 or was that 40? Yes, it is 40?"

I looked at him curiously and asked, "Where exactly is it in the cargo bay"?

"Uh! Just go down to the cargo bay and look around, you should find it." (He paused again) "I mean, you will find it there?" (This time the pause was a bit longer), "I think?", he answered. (Obviously being human was not necessarily an improvement.)

Chapter 3
THE CARGO BAY

AFTER REACHING THE BULKHEAD MARKED Q-3345; I used the card that George gave me. Once inside I tried to look for that box but the illumination in the cargo bay was very poor. When my eyes finally adjusted, I could see everything in the cargo bay, except that box.

After looking around awhile I did find the box completely on the opposite side of the cargo bay! I checked the invoice number against the label ID number to see if this was the right box. I also speculated how someone so vague was in charge of a cargo office.

The *cargo bay shook.* I landed on the floor. It felt like the outpost itself had been hit by some hot shot space jockey who had no clue how to dock in a docking bay.

I got up and ran for the bulkhead. I ran a short distance before I felt the artificial gravity fail. I found myself floating up towards the cargo bay doors. I went up only a few meters before someone restored the artificial gravity. I landed a bit hard, and I fell backwards striking my head on the floor. I was knocked unconscious. I think I was out for only a few minutes. When I came to I saw things around me in the cargo bay floating up towards the doors in the ceiling.

I heard an alarm blaring in a strange language. At first it was hard for me to understand, but the more I listened to the warning the easier it was to understand. As the warning was repeated over and over, gradually the meaning became apparent. "Hull breach in ten, no five minutes, evacuate the cargo bay before decompression." I was not really sure about the time because the numbers were not always easy to translate correctly. However, I knew that I had to get out of the cargo bay as soon as possible.

As I ran towards the bulkhead in the cargo bay I also looked around for any other ways of getting out. Blast it. If the captain really wanted this box that badly, he should get it for himself. I really did not want to die on this outpost if I could help it.

I quickly put on my oxygen mask, the one piece of equipment that no one who works in space is ever without. It supposedly gives you enough oxygen to reach safety. I had never had to try it out. At the same time the cargo bay doors in the ceiling began to open slowly because of the hull breach. Suddenly, I found myself being sucked up towards the cargo bay doors, so I grabbed hold of the nearest steel tie ring on the floor. The tie rings looked to be about 2 inches in diameter.

I struggled, trying not to get sucked up through the opening cargo bay doors. I was hit in the leg by a box, which almost made me lose my grip on the floor ring. I kicked the box away; it struck the floor and flew open. I looked inside and found what looked like a space suit. I grabbed it and put it on. Hopefully, I could get out of the cargo bay alive and catch a ride back to the ship even though I didn't have that box.

Putting the suit on without getting sucked out the cargo bay doors was a major problem. I put my foot through a floor ring anchoring myself to the floor. Struggling into the space suit I found it was too tight. Working frantically, I took off my uniform and put the spacesuit back on. It was a tight fit but it would work.

I looked around for the helmet and I did not see it anywhere. As I looked up toward the doors in the ceiling I did notice something shiny. I focused on the small shiny object which I fervently hoped was the helmet to the suit I was wearing.

With one giant effort I bent down as much as I could and pushed off the floor as hard as I could to propel myself up and out of the cargo hole. I had to get the helmet and put it on. I wouldn't last much longer without it. The oxygen in my mask wasn't going to last longer than a few more minutes.

When I reached the helmet, I took one long last deep breath from the oxygen bottle then took the mask off. I grabbed the helmet, put it on my head and turned it. I heard the rush of oxygen flowing in.

I slowly spun around, there was a bright flash. As I tried to correct myself I saw a few of the canisters escape from the ties, float up and collide with the cargo bay doors. The explosion was strong enough to rip an enormous hole in the cargo bay and blow me further out into space.

"Milroy, where were you when the cargo bay exploded?" Gilroy interrupted.

"I had just ordered Kilos to unlock from the outpost. The others were back. Where was Joneb? Did he get the vaccine? It was an agonizing time."

"Gilroy, shall I continue?" He nodded.

"I tried to get the radio and the internal suit light to work. A few minutes later I was hit in the back by something. When I turned, I saw a black transfer disk. I looked a little farther and saw that box of vaccine."

"With the force of that explosion I had just enough time to grab the disk and the box. Then

I floated until I was clear of the debris. I used the disk to get back to the ship."

I did finally get the radio to work. I called the ship. Boy was I glad to hear Jonroy's voice! It took me a moment or two to figure out the disk I was standing on. It was more responsive than I expected. Although I tried to stop all I did was slam into the bulkhead. But then they did open the door.

"When I opened the air lock, the captain was waiting. Boy did he look mad. 'It's about time you got back here. I thought you might have floated home!' Someone laughed nervously at the captain's remark. He looked around, quickly silencing any further outbursts, and then continued. 'Where did you get that spacesuit? Where is your uniform? What took you so long to get this box to me? Did you know it has been several hours since I sent you on that simple task?'" he spoke forcefully with a bite to his words.

"No sir I didn't know. I was too busy trying

to stay alive. Without the spacesuit I never would have survived. I had to sacrifice the uniform. I said defensively as I paused. He raised an eyebrow. "Now if you will excuse me sir, I will go change and report back to the bridge."

"'*NO*, I will not excuse you,' the captain said abruptly. '*NOT* until you tell me why it took you so long to get me this box of vaccine?'"

"The First Officer came up behind the captain and quietly spoke, 'The vaccine, sir. Remember, we need to get it to your brother.'"

"'Right, right,' the captain said as he lifted his hand in recognition. 'You have one hour! Then I want to know why it took you so long to get me this box and why the cargo bay exploded!'"

"'Confine him to his quarters Mister Kilo', the Captain ordered."

"'Let's go.' The First Officer said, marching me to my quarters." The walk was long and very quiet!

"'Sit down.'"

But sir, I need to at least get out of this suit."

"All right, get cleaned up quickly!" Standing at attention he glared at me.

I changed quickly into appropriate gear and sat down without a word. He was still glaring at me. The hour passed slowly. The intercom buzzed. 'Bring him to the mess hall.'"

"'Yes, sir.'" The First Officer replied. He let me leave the room first. When we walked to the mess hall he kept me in front. We walked in almost total silence except for the occasional voice heard when we passed a cabin. It was like a ghost ship."

"We reached the mess hall and stepped inside. The landing crew stood at the back wall. I looked around for the captain. I saw him sitting in a chair in the middle of a long table. It was hard to see who else was sitting at the table but I could see that there were at least two others. I was sitting in a chair under a spotlight. I wasn't sure who they were. When Captain Milroy started the inquiry, I recognized them."

"The two crew members were Kilos (Navigational

Officer) and Rojas (communication officer). I was not sure why they were sitting with the captain but I hoped that it was good for me."

"After I sat down, the First Officer walked to the table in order to sit down but the captain motioned to him. They conferred quietly. The First Officer stood up and left the room. I tried to catch a glimpse of the First Officer's face but the light was too dim. I couldn't determine if things were good or bad."

"So, I looked back to the captain and he looked at me, a curious look on his face. 'Well, we're waiting.'"

"I started my report but the captain stopped me. 'Not too much detail.' I continued my report making my remarks concise."

When I finished, I heard the door open behind me. I looked at the captain; he motioned to someone to come forward. As the person passed me I looked up and saw it was the First Officer. He walked up to the head table and gave the captain a report pad.

The captain glanced at the pad and appeared to be a bit surprised."

"He had a slight grin on his face 'This report and your crewmate's statements substantiate what you have told me. You did all you could to get this box to me.' He paused then continued, 'Nor did you cause the explosion that destroyed the cargo bay at the outpost.'"

"He said, 'Stand up.' I jumped to my feet. He continued, 'You have been reinstated to full active duty. This is conditional on verification of certain details from the Durban outpost.'"

"Thank you, sir, I said a few times. I saluted him, turned around and walked out of the mess hall and returned to the bridge."

"A few hours later we arrived at Argyle. We had barely touched down at the hospital landing pad. When the Captain pushed the hatch door open and run into the hospital. And that's my story."

"That is a very interesting story Joneb. And Milroy, you can corroborate his story?"

"Most of it."

"So, how much, Milroy?"

"Fitzroy and the landing party did confirm that he met up with them inside the outpost. And the pad that Kilo gave me had other information on it to confirm that Joneb did go to the office. As far as the incident in the cargo bay, we have only his word. I hope to have that confirmed by the surveillance cameras in the cargo bay."

"But weren't they damaged when the cargo bay was destroyed?" I asked.

"Yes, Joneb they were but only after the second explosion. I've made contact with someone on the outpost and they agreed to send me a copy of that recording as soon as they determine that Joneb is innocent and the recording doesn't have any other information on it they might need."

"Now I want to see father and get some dinner. I haven't eaten well lately. I was worried even before I got Gilroy's message. I sensed there was something wrong. I didn't know what it was. It's been a nerve wracking period."

There was a long silence. It was only broken by the sound of an alarm. "What is that?" Milroy asked.

"That's only the videophone." Said Fitzroy. "Dad, I thought you were going to get a new one?"

"You moved out so why should I. Now that I spend more time at the hospital I don't need one." Gilroy got up and answered the videophone. "This is Doctor Gilroy. How may I help you?"

"Your father is awake and he is asking for you and your brother."

"Thank you, we'll be right there."

Gilroy looked at Milroy. "Come on let's go."

"But Gilroy, I want to wait for that information."

"Yes, I know but Dad wants to see us."

"You guys go. I'll wait here for the information. When it comes I will come to the hospital? I'll find you and give you the information." Said Upjon.

"Thank you Upjon."

"Okay, then let's go." Said Gilroy.

We walked towards the door. When Fitzroy opened the door, there was a messenger outside with his hand up as if he were going to knock on the door. "Who are you and how may we help you?" Asked Fitzroy.

"I have a package from the security office on the Durban outpost. I was told the information was needed for a trial."

"Hey, Uncle, there's a courier here for you. I think he has the information you're waiting for."

"Oh! Good. Let me through." Milroy got to the door. Looking at the courier, he asks. "Where do I sign?"

"Right here. Sir." The courier pointed at the dotted line on the flimsy plastic and handed him a stylus.

Milroy looked up at the courier and said, "Thank you." Then he looked at his brother and said, "Okay Gilroy let's go and see father. I will read this on the way."

We all got in to Gilroy's shuttle and lifted off for the hospital. I sat across from the captain.

The Captain sat there, examining the message. Occasionally, he glanced at me or his brother. Finally, I couldn't stand it any longer. Looking at the Captain I asked, "Well, what does it say?"

The Captain looked up at me then back down at the flimsy plastic. "I see by this report that it wasn't you that caused the explosion which surprises me. Yes, you might be innocent of just trying to survive but as far as my Niece goes you are quite taken with her. When I asked Rojas if what I suspected was true she acknowledged that she is interested in you too. Just so you know, on this planet we expect any attachments to be honored completely."

He shook his head and looked back down at the flimsy plastic and remarked. "It was a hot shot jockey pilot that started a chain reaction by slamming into the side of the spaceport. Then he tried to get himself free by putting his engines into reverse. By doing so he ripped a hole in the refueling pipes. You are completely exonerated."

We landed at the hospital. Gilroy and Milroy went see their father. I breathed a sigh of relief. Dinner plans were under way. We would meet at the restaurant down the street. I was looking forward to meeting the rest of the family. It had certainly been an interesting introduction to this half of the family. In spite of everything, I was looking forward to being on a new planet with friends and the possibility of becoming a part of the family. Little did I realize just how that would happen.

Chapter 4

ARGYLE

ROJAS GRABBED ME AS THE crew started separating, relaxing as the immediate crisis dissipated. "Come on, I want to show you something. She led the way down a side road, trees on either side. After a short walk, we came to a bench with a view of the lake I had seen earlier. "Sit down and listen," she commanded.

I sat down and waited expectantly. She twisted her hands a bit, then started to talk. "I hope you didn't take my uncle's remarks the wrong way. I do like you but I don't want to make a long-term commitment yet. These agreements are considered very sacred on Argyle and are not to be entered into lightly. It's also hard on a small ship like the Star Struck to have an intimate relationship."

I grabbed her hands and squeezed them gently. I kissed each hand gently. Then I looked her straight in the eyes and almost lost my resolve not to go any further. However, after a moment, I spoke quietly, "oh my sweet Rojas, you are very special to me. I don't want to lose you. I promise to give you time. But first, I leaned over and gave her a long, kiss. She hesitated briefly, then responded fully, enjoying the moment completely. Then she broke off, giving me a blindingly beautiful smile.

"That's much better," she said. "Now let's go get some food. I'm starving."

"Me too" I replied, although I would have liked to spend more time with her alone.

When we reached the town, we headed for the Rancheria, a bright, cheerful spot where the wait staff wore colorful skirts or pants in bright shades of reds, blues and gold, which contrasted strikingly with their white shirts. Music played in the background with a toe tapping rhythm. It was a great place, with a light atmosphere and a nice sense of companionship among the people. We saw Jonroy, David and Raymond at a table for six. They waved us over. "Come on, we saved you a seat," Jonroy said. "Jacson is joining us later. Upjon decided to go see his friend, Debora. They have kept in touch since he joined our crew."

She paused briefly, then spoke so quietly, we all leaned forward to listen to her. "It was so strange when we stopped to get the vaccine" she whispered, "almost as if we had enemies."

"Jonroy," Rojas said, "this is not the place for this conversation!" She looked up, laughing as the waiter came to the table. "Yes, bring us two of the shellfish specials and a couple of home brews."

"I know that you will like what I ordered, Joneb. They make the best shellfish dinners in town."

"And it makes a great change from space chow," Jonroy added. "You are right, of course, Rojas."

Our conversation remained light. We talked about different species we had encountered in our travels. When the food came, I couldn't help but agree that it was delicious.

Chapter 5
FAMILY BUSINESS

Meanwhile, Milroy and Gilroy had gone into see their father, Kilroy. Gilroy of course, checked all of the readings and medical information that was available before going in. Seeing his father, in bed, looking pale and listless, made Milroy realize just how close they had come to losing him. He struggled to stay calm, although he was ready to take on all their opponents at once.

"Calm down", their father commanded. Even though he was weak, he still had enough character to make them sit down quickly and at attention.

"Now listen to me. We have some things to discuss to bring things to a good conclusion. It's taken me a while but I have news of our women!

"What?" Milroy and Gilroy spoke almost in unison. "I had almost given up hope of ever finding Junaray," said Milroy. Gilroy echoed his sentiments about Marona, his wife.

"It took me a while and I had to call in a few

favors, but I finally found them. They are in the desert on the Genesis outpost. There is a settlement there where they are treated well but are unable to leave." He leaned back against the bed, tired but happy to have such good news.

"It won't be easy but I think we can visit the settlement under pretense of wanting to make it our home and then smuggle them out when we leave. Gilroy, you will have to go since Mamaroy may need your services on the trip home."

"You mean Mama is alive?" Milroy and Gilroy almost shouted with relief.

"Shhh!!!" "we can't be too careful," Kilroy emphasized with a look. It will take all your skills to get to Genesis, spring the women and return here without any trouble." "As it is, you will need to be careful of the Mackelray clan." "I don't have proof but I think they were behind the abduction of our women. They wanted the interplanetary contract very badly."

"Dad" began Milroy, "I don't think you are

right about the Mackelrays. Willison and I have always been friends even though you and his Dad could never see eye to eye." "I think we have a bigger enemy-the Planetary Alliance. They want a monopoly on space travel contracts even when it is only a small one like ours. I keep trying to find out who is backing them but they are quick to hide that information. However, they had the connections to set up the abductions and move the women to the Genesis system, something the Mackelrays would not have been able to do."

"Maybe you are right, son," Kilroy conceded. "But you must be careful. Send in this new kid, Joneb, Upjon, Raymond and David. Maybe Jacson if he would be a help. Their faces are not so well known."

"You should stay another day and leave at 2nd moonrise. We could fake a message for a delivery in the Quad sector with a request for a Doctor to help with a medical outpost for a short period. That would explain Gilroy's presence."

Milroy and Gilroy thought things through. They looked at each other and gave a nod. "I will contact a friend to send me a message about the medical outpost needs," Gilroy said.

Milroy added, "I will set up a delivery request as well. And alert the crew about our plans." "Can I stay here over night with Dad??"

Gilroy nodded. "Stay here until breakfast, then make the arrangements you need. But first, go get something to eat. I will stay until you get back."

Milroy headed out to the nearest eatery and ordered takeout. Taking out his communicator, he called Kilo. "Meet me at our usual spot" he said cryptically.

About 30 minutes later, they met. There was a bench in a park nearby but Milroy bypassed it to walk to a lesser used walkway. They sat for a short period listening quietly. When Milroy was satisfied that no one was within earshot, he filled Kilo in. He asked him to put in the request for supplies from the Quad Sector and spread the news to the crew about pulling out the next day at 2nd moonrise. Milroy headed back to the hospital feeling refreshed. He settled down on a chair in his Dad's room and Gilroy headed home.

Meanwhile, Kilo met up with the group at the Rancheria. "Hey guys, how's the food?"

"Great Kilo" "What's up?" asked Rojas, shooting a look at Joneb.

"Just the usual in station stuff. Look, we are going to be here overnight. Then we take off again at 2nd moonrise."

Rojas looked surprised, then shrugged her shoulders. "I thought we would be here longer this time".

"Such is the life of space ship crews," Kilo simply replied. "Look, I'm going to contact the rest of the crew and let them know. I'll bunk down on the ship." With a casual wave, he headed off towards the spaceport.

Joneb looked at Rojas and said, "I take it this is a little unusual."

Rojas looked uncomfortable, "Not now, Joneb."
"Let's head home and get some rest,".

"That sounds good." Everyone got up and headed out.

Rojas and Jonroy walked together for a little while, David, Raymond and I brought up the rear. As we left the brightly lit area, a group rushed us. All of a sudden, we were in the middle of a fight. Someone got off a kick in my stomach just as I was trying to get someone off of Rojas. David and Raymond fought off their attackers and the girls managed some defensive moves we didn't know they had. Just as suddenly, as reinforcements from the town joined us, our assailants took off. "Is everyone okay?" Kilos demanded. A quick assessment verified that everyone was accounted for and mostly unhurt. Thanking the town group, Kilos rounded us up and directed us to the space ship. "I think we'll be safer there," he said circumspectly. There are too many spacers in town right now. Back on the space ship, he ordered us to our quarters and lights out by 2300 hours. So, after talking a little bit and doing the needed first aid for our cuts and bruises, we were all in our bunks by curfew.

I lay awake, thinking things over, trying to make sense of the fight but feeling as if I didn't have enough information. I was also wondering if this family had secrets I would need to know to survive.

In the morning, I discovered we were restricted to the ship. Anyone still off ship would have to wait until sundown to come on board. Little pockets of conversation would start up only to die down quickly if someone else ventured nearby. It seemed like a long day, with no one wanting to ask questions but still wanting to know what was up. Finally, everyone was on board, supper was served and we were coming up on 2nd moonrise which was our departure time. Everyone was surprised to see Gilroy come on board and put his gear in the Captain's room. The Captain announced General

Quarters and then said there would be a staff meeting at 20:30 hours after we were off plant.

We all assembled in the mess hall at the appointed hour. Captain Milroy started off by addressing the family members, telling them the good news about Mamaroy, Junaray, and Marona. Yes, they had been found and were doing well. However, getting them off planet was going to be tricky and would involve some planning. He asked Upjon, Raymond, David and myself to stay for a strategy meeting. Jonroy spoke up. "Sir, I think Rojas and I should be in on this meeting.

It would be helpful and I can handle myself in any situation."

Milroy responded, "Certainly not. It's too risky. I won't have it."

Jonroy shot back, "if we are going to gain the settlers' trust, they will expect to see women in the party. They will not want single men settling with them. I could go as Raymond's partner and Rojas could go as Joneb's partner."

"Certainly not," Gilroy answered.

"You know we have to if the plan is to succeed," the girls responded.

"You're right but we don't like it." The fathers nodded together, briefly talking. "All right, now does anyone know anything about these desert nomads?"

David spoke up—"is this the Genesis settlement?"

"Yes," replied the Captain.

"They are a close bunch, but fair and honest in their dealings." He thought a few minutes. "They might have bought the women from their captives or have agreed to hold them for a price. Either way, we would need to expect to give them a price for the women. The settlement is too isolated to sneak in and out easily or to smuggle anyone out. We have a lot of trade goods that we could bargain with. Add in some Central Credits that are good in this part of the system and we should be good to go. Rojas and Jonroy should dress down, wear pants with tunic tops and have dust veils. They also need to act meek and not talk out of turn. They should not draw attention to themselves. This is a male dominated world and it can be harsh and arbitrary in judgments. We should be able to rent a shifter craft for our party. Joneb and I should be in charge. Raymond will be our assistant. Otherwise his accent might be questioned."

By now, with a few false trails laid out, we had reversed our course to head towards the Genesis settlement. Everyone turned in, but I doubt many of us really slept, between the news and the plans, everyone was keyed up, both excited and daunted by the scope of the plan.

Chapter 6

THE GENESIS SETTLEMENT

DAVID AND I LED THE way down the ramp to the dock port. Raymond followed with a slurry full of trade goods. We strolled over to the dock port to look at possible shifters. David saw one that belonged to a former acquaintance. I was strolling over to the vendor when someone bumped into me, mumbled an apology and hurried off in the other direction. I tried to keep going without showing any unexpected emotion but the truth was, I was flabbergasted! If I was not mistaken, I had just come across an old pal, the sort that will back you up in a fight. Why was he here and why had he given me a warning? Years ago, we had established a warning signal on planets far away that had served us well in many tight situations. I wrenched my thoughts back to the present and wandered over to David. He was haggling over the price of the shifter, so I didn't interrupt. Finally, they were done and we attached the slurry to the back of the shifter. David had done well, we had a covered shifter with dust shields on the side. Not only did that keep us from prying eyes, but it also helped keep the ever-present dust out of the vehicles.

Meanwhile, Jonroy and Rojas had stayed away from the shifter stalls since women were not plentiful in this area. Instead they had gone to the food tents and purchased a few snacks, some fruit and a container of water. We did not expect to be long but it was wise to be prepared.

As we were climbing into the vehicle, a messenger boy ran up to me, handed me an envelope and took off before I could say anything. David looked at me quizzically, but I told him to go. So, we headed out the long dusty trail that led to Mantray, the desert settlement.

Looking down at the envelope, I opened it. It showed a place with a water hole with an x marking it. It gave a time to stop there along with the distinctive mark of my friend. So I directed David to the coordinates. Rojas looked at me with a question but I shook my head. Time enough to share this when I had the full explanation. My friend, Marcus was a good ally but I didn't know why he was even in this quadrant of space.

Reaching our rendezvous point, I got out and wandered over to the other side of the water hole. Marcus stepped out of the shadows and looked at me.

"Man, oh man!" he exclaimed. "You do manage to land in the middle of things!"

"What do you mean?" I asked.

"I've been looking into the Planetary Alliance and their dealings in this quadrant of space. They have used intimidation tactics in a number of small settlements including your friends here. We have found out that they are setting a trap for the Kilroy clan with the women as bait."

"So, what are we going to do? We can't turn back now. And who are you working with?"

"That's not really important. But here is my plan. Gilroy should return in disguise to my ship with my crew. Then, once we are on our way back from Mantray, Gilroy will send a message to Milroy with a rendezvous point on another planet. My crew will provide assistance and cover after we leave Mantray. With luck, we should all get out of here in one piece."

We walked back to the shifter. I could feel the questions shouting at me even though everyone was quiet. "This is my friend, Marcus. I have worked with him before and he is a good man to have in a fight. He has information that we are heading into an ambush and some ideas to get us out of here with a minimum of trouble."

He nodded. He explained briefly that he would impersonate Gilroy, who would go back to his ship, with a message to send to Milroy with rendezvous coordinates two days from now.

Everyone started talking at once. "Silence!" Gilroy said. "I know a little about the Planetary Alliance and they are ruthless. They would think nothing about killing us all rather than letting us succeed. How do you think you can outrun them?"

"Simple", stated Marcus. "We are going to stage an accident, one that they will have no trouble believing. We don't have much time. You have stopped here the maximum amount of time. Any more delays and you will have too many questions."

Reluctantly, Gilroy got out. Immediately, Marcus' team came out of the shadows and motioned him over to their transport. This was a much faster vehicle than our little shifter and was semi-airborne so it left no tracks.

We headed onward to Mantray, Marcus continued to discuss strategy on the way. "Remember, my name is Gilroy, Dad or Uncle Gilroy. I am here to lend medical aid to the settlement."

The bleak landscape echoed my thoughts. There were grey and blue cactus-like plants here and there, with occasional tumbleweeds rolling around in the dust. Occasional quick slithers hinted of snakes or lizard like animals that live in desert areas. The pale sun was heating up the interior of the shifter. Still we were quiet.

As we drew nearer the settlement, Marcus gave us one last reminder: "Joneb and I will do most of the talking. Take your cue from us. If at any time, you hear a sharp whistle, followed by the word, 'Scramble!' move as quickly as you can to the shifter. Defend yourselves if needed and get going. If I am not there, take off anyway, with as many as can make it. My crew will be waiting for you."

We came to a halt in front of the primary building in Mantray. The headman came out. "Welcome to Mantray, state your names and your business."

"I am Joneb from Gonargh. My brothers and I are thinking of settling here. We have heard good things about Mantray."

"I am Gilroy. I understand there are medical needs here."

"You are right," the headman motioned to an assistant. "Take the Doctor over to the Medical Tent. Brief him on the situation. I will talk to Joneb myself." Marcus had acquired a dust jacket which had a hood. Pulling the hood up over his head, he followed the assistant across the compound. Motioning to me, the headman said, "The rest of your party can wait in the courtyard. My women will bring them some drinks." With a glance at Rojas, I followed the headman into the building. Raymond checked that the rest went to the covered tent in the courtyard, but a quick word with David sent him back to the shifter. Raymond caught up with us as we were going inside. Although the building and town seemed primitive, all the communicators and vid screens seemed very much up to date. I glanced around, pretending awe at everything.

My name is Jamson, the headman said. "how big is your group?"

"There are 8 of us not counting the women." I replied and some of us need women. I understand you could possibly help us with that, with compensation of course."

"Yes, of course, said Jamson smoothly. "Perhaps you would like to look at our selection later."

"Ah, here we are. Please have a glass of our special orange water. It is very refreshing."

"Thank you. How is the farming here? Do you irrigate or use hydroponics?"

"It is a combination of both techniques, depending on the crop."

We continued talking about the settlement for a while, then he invited me to see the women. "Bring your assistant along also," he added as an afterthought.

Going into the courtyard, I glanced over at our group. Everything seemed calm but I was feeling uneasy. Things were just a little too quiet. We followed Jamson across the town.

I cautioned Raymond not to show any emotion. There were about a dozen women in the food tent. Some were involved in food preparation, others were cleaning and others were washing clothes. None of them looked up. Almost immediately,

I noticed a woman who must have been Rojas' mother. Even at a quick glance, I could see the resemblance. Looking around, I saw a woman assisting an older woman with her duties. I sensed that they were Mamaroy and Junaray. Continuing to follow Jamson, I signaled him. "We could use 3 women to help us in our move. Perhaps these women."

"Are you sure? We've had some problems with this group."

"Oh, that will be no problem. We have ways of controlling our women--without violence of course.", I added with a knowing glance at the headman.

"Of course," Jamson sneered. "I think you will fit in well here." We bickered a little on the price and then we signed the agreement. Jamson pushed a few buttons, we transferred the credits; then the women were summoned, given traveling clothes and led out the door by a stunned Raymond. The women didn't say a word, simply shuffled along, crying silently and without a backwards glance. Another woman screamed, 'No, it will kill her!" as her partner shushed her.

I was halfway across the compound when I heard it. A shrill whistle, followed by Scramble! Raymond and the women were almost to the shuttle when the fighting started. Quickly, I closed the distance to the shifter, "In, IN, IN!" I yelled, practically throwing the whole crew in. David had finally managed to start the shifter. Frantically, I struggled to release the slurry. One last knot, a quick push off and the shifter was finally on its way. I dove in the side falling onto Raymond. Suddenly, I realized that Marcus was not with us. Hopefully, he would rejoin us down the road, knowing full well, that he usually managed to extricate himself from the stickiest situations. Glancing back, I noticed smoke coming from one of the tents. As we sped down the road as fast as we could, I noticed 3 speed cars taking up pursuit. One was just a little bit ahead of the others. I could only hope it was Marcus making his escape and also covering our tracks.

Suddenly, David jerked the shifter to the side and headed off in a southerly direction. "What are you doing?" I roared, clinging to the seat strap. "Are you out of your mind?"

"Look back there" he said yelling to be heard over everyone's cries and exclamations.

Looking over my shoulder, I saw a big planetary gunship bearing down on us. "Get down" I yelled, cursing as I pulled open the weapon stash. I distributed them to Raymond and the others. "Don't fire until I give the word." Quickly I spoke with David, "keep going for 5 more minutes and then let the engine sputter and die".

He looked at me startled, thinking I was nuts. Then he nodded and floored the pedal. After a few minutes, the shifter started faltering, its motion, bumpy and uneven. All of a sudden, we jarred to a stop.

I stepped down motioning the others to stay

in the shifter. "Keep the weapons out of sight." I cautioned as I looked behind us. Mine was behind my back. A few men came off of the gunship and started to approach. I knew that the captain of the gunship had guns trained on us so I held my hands forward, palms out and walked towards them.

"Greetings," the second in command said with a small smile. "Are you lost or do you have a problem with your shifter?"

"A little of both," I replied. "My driver said there was a problem with the steering. Shortly after that the engine started sputtering. We barely managed to hold on the last few minutes. We just came from the Mantray settlement and now I have no idea where the spaceport is."

I waited nervously while he reported to his captain. Then he asked, "there seemed to be an explosion at Mantray right when you left. What can you tell me about that?"

Thinking quickly, I replied, "I don't have any idea. We were getting into the shifter after we had concluded our business when we heard a commotion. We have a deadline for our departure and left before anything happened."

"What was your business at Mantray?" he asked.

"Oh, we had heard that Mantray is a good place for families to settle. So we negotiated over settlement and also acquired some women to help with our move. It was mutually beneficial for both parties." I smiled, a small, meaningful smile I hoped would indicate I was just a simple future settler.

After a few agonizing minutes, the sergeant looked over at the shifter. "You know, we could give you a lift back to the spaceport," he offered offhandedly.

"No thanks," I said. "We appreciate the support, but our driver is very good with shifters". There was no way I wanted to put us in jeopardy. Once we boarded that gunship, we would be at their mercy and would probably never see daylight again. I wasn't sure how we were going to get out of this situation, but I was hoping that Marcus and his crew were nearby.

I walked over to the shifter and motioned to David. "Pretend to be looking at the engine, fiddle with things, like you are going to fix it." He nodded. I motioned the rest out the other side of the shifter, handing Raymond a shovel. "Dig out that front wheel, as quickly as you can." Looking at me questioningly, I simply shrugged and grabbed a shovel. "Hey you" speaking to Rojas. "Get a bota of water out and make sure everyone gets a drink." She nodded, with her eyes to the ground. She brought it first to me as the head of the group and then to Raymond and David.

There was enough for the rest of the women. I dug out the other wheel and looked at David. A half hour had passed.

He stood up and said, "time to try it out."

I strolled over and tried to start it up. A couple of false starts, but then, David touched something on the engine and it started on the next try. I knew that he had disconnected something to cause this, but didn't say anything, quietly hoping the gunship captain would accept our explanation. I motioned everyone back in the shifter and went to speak to the sergeant.

He met me halfway, looking at the shifter. "Looks like you were right. Now before you go on your way, we need a fee from you."

I groaned inwardly. Hopefully this wouldn't be too big a "fee". "How much," I asked, "and why weren't we told beforehand?"

"You were supposed to be told when you rented the shifter. We are always having this problem with these shifter owners. They charge you the fee but then 'forget' to give it us. Then, we have to charge you double the fee."

"OK, okay," I said. "What is the fee?"

"Five Thousand credits," or we could take 2 of your women instead," he added casually.

I breathed a small sigh of relief since we did have enough to pay the fee. "I am tempted but we need the women for our move. However, I may have to rethink our move if these fees are part of living here."

"Relax, friend, you will find that these fees are for off worlders only."

An assistant brought the credit transfer cube over, we concluded the transaction and the gunship headed on its way.

"Let's get a move on. Head for the watering hole."

David looked at me, "which way?"

At that moment, I caught a glimpse of movement off to the right. Before I could even grab my weapon, both Jonroy and Rojas had their weapons pointed at the solitary man running up to the shifter. He stopped abruptly, throwing back his hood. "I began to think you were going to have a party with them," Marcus said. Nodding at the two girls, he stepped in and said, "head east for 5 minutes."

"Man, oh man!" I took a deep breath. "I had almost written you off. What happened?"

"Not now, we are not out of danger yet! When we get to the watering hole, everyone stay alert!" Our mood altered. We had started to relax and feel a sense of elation. His caution restored the tension as well as the watchfulness of everyone.

Everyone was quiet, reflecting on the harrowing events and waiting for the next crisis. I reached over and squeezed Rojas hand. She squeezed mine back and gave a small smile.

"Everyone listen up," Marcus said abruptly. "When we stop at the watering hole, we are going to stage an accident. My men will be there with the needed tools for sabotage. You will do exactly what I say without questions. Is that clear?"

Everyone nodded somberly. Nobody looked around, the three women drew closer together, lending needed support to the older woman.

"Now I need your outer garments," speaking to the five women. "What!?" Rojas spoke up quickly, snapping her mouth shut quickly when Marcus glared at her. "We will have replacement clothes on our spinner when we are all done. Now, quickly!" The women quietly removed their outer garments, handing them to Raymond and me. "The rest of you give me your jackets."

The evening sun was starting down the horizon as we came to a stop at the watering hole. No sooner had we stopped than Marcus' spinner glided over and men jumped out quickly. They grabbed the clothes and went back on board. Shortly after that they came out carrying bodies which were wearing our clothes.

Horrified, I looked at Marcus and wondered what lengths he had gone to for this. Seeing my look, he shook his head and murmured a small "Later".

Motioning to the women, he waved them over to the spinner where a ramp had appeared and men were waiting to help them aboard. All of a sudden, a large man came over and picked up Mamaroy gently and walked up into the spinner. The others quickly followed.

"Now, David, back her up a little and run her into that collection of brush over there, really fast like she was out of control".

"But," David started to say.

"It will be all right," Marcus said encouragingly. "Quickly now, we don't have much time".

David hopped in, backed up and rammed the ship into the brush. He stepped out looking dazed and slightly confused. Raymond, with a nod at Marcus, led him up the ramp.

"All right boys," Marcus yelled, "stage the bodies and set the charges." A few minutes passed and then the word went around—clear out! Everyone rushed up the ramp which closed just as a big whomp shook the shifter. We could smell the fumes and see a little of the smoke from the wreck. Marcus spoke in a mike to the pilot and the spinner moved back and forth over the area, the wind from the spinner smoothing away any footprints. Then we headed back toward the spaceport.

Chapter 7

HEADING FOR FREEDOM

I LOOKED AROUND THE SPINNER, LOCATING Rojas and Jonroy, then the other women. As promised, they had on new clothing and the three were being served some sort of soup broth and crackers. Nobody spokes very much, things had happened too quickly. It was hard to believe we had come this far. Most everyone was in shock.

As for myself, I knew from experience that I would deal with my feelings later on—right now I needed to know the next steps. Looking around I saw Marcus talking with the man who carried Mamaroy into the ship. I found out later, he was their medic and recognized that Mamaroy was close to collapse. I crossed over to Marcus and said, "We need to talk."

Looking at me, he said, "Right. Follow me." He led the way into a small room and closed the door.

Raising a hand, he stopped my questions before I could even ask them. "Milroy has left the planet.

He got the message from Gilroy and will meet us in two days' time. In the meantime, we are altering our course. It will appear that we are returning from the other settlement. We will have a few crates of materials which we have bought to go on board our ship. The 3 women will be taken over in the crates. This is the only way we can do it without drawing any attention to them. We will sedate the older woman so she won't be traumatized by the experience. In fact, we put the sedative in her soup so she should be asleep by now. Jonroy and Rojas can dress like members of my crew and no one will know the difference. You need to tell them not to speak to anyone, just grunt, point, carry their load and get on board. They will appear as any menial member of the crew and therefore, not important enough to hassle. They will not like it but it is imperative they do as I say. Everyone's safety depends on it."

Rojas had been watching the door and descended on me as soon as I stepped out. She was frantic with worry because Mamaroy was asleep and seemed very fragile. I quickly outlined the plan and she just looked at me with disbelief.

"How could you do this to them. They won't be able to handle it! I won't let him do it—"

I grabbed her fist which she was shaking in my face. "My dear Rojas".

"I am NOT your Rojas!" she hissed at me.

"Shut up then," I whispered back. "You are not a silly person. This is the way it must be done. Every effort will be made to ensure their comfort. It will be all right."

"But," she began.

"Hush daughter" her mother came up to us. "Listen to him".

"But Mother" she began again trembling.

"No," her mother spoke again. "We have come too far to turn back. We will do as he says. Mamaroy is tough, she will make it."

"All right, Mother." Rojas turned from me refusing to look at me.

"Give her time, my son, give her time". Marona gave me a reassuring look.

Looking at her, I said, "how did you know?"

"Mothers always know." She replied as she crossed the room to the rest of the family.

Preparations were made to ensure the three women's comfort in the crates. They were then placed gently on a shifter bed to be ferried over to the space ship. The rest of us put on our disguises and kept quiet.

Marcus came over to me. "Just a quick word— David may not be who he seems."

Startled, I looked at him. He nodded. "We knew one of the group was a plant but were unable to figure out which one." He spoke quietly so only I was able to hear him. "We will take care of him on the way over to the ship." I nodded thoughtfully.

"Just roll with the punches."

"Okay." I felt like I was riding a huge wave on one of the water worlds - tumbling over and over again.

We came to rest in the main center of the spaceport just like anyone coming in from the other settlement.

As the ramp went down, I heard Marcus yelling orders to the crew. "I want everything moved over to our ship orderly and carefully."

As the crew picked up their loads, a shifter transport bed came over and the crates were slid over carefully. The transport then left with a crew member to go to the Wandering Moon. The rest of us picked up our loads and lumbered after them. As we were walking over, one of Marcus' men stumbled and fell sideways knocking David over, both men went down. Quickly, two men from the crew picked them both up laughing at the man who had tripped. "Man, you tripped over your own two feet again," they said as they helped a stunned David to his feet. He was walking but didn't seem really aware of his surroundings. I quickly picked up the spilled load and hurried after them. Gradually everyone filed on board. Marcus was the last one in and the door quickly slid into place. "We take off in 30 minutes," he said. "Grab a seat and strap in". He went forward to the pilot's seat and sat down next to his co-pilot. I looked around noticing that David was already strapped in his seat and still looked dazed.

Rojas and Jonroy grabbed 2 seats together and the others sat wherever they could. I sat down near the crates to keep an eye on them. The tension in the ship was high. At last, we heard Marcus asking for clearance from the spaceport. There was a collective sigh of relief from everyone as we lifted off.

We had to rise into the upper atmosphere before we could begin to orbit. At last we were free from the planet's gravity and heading to an unknown destination. Hopefully, we would meet Milroy there and head home.

Once we got the all clear, we concentrated on releasing the three women. Mamaroy was released first and carried to a bunk where the Doctor examined her. "She will be all right after some rest." There was a little reservation in his voice which alerted me to the possibility that she might not be in good condition. Looking around, I didn't think anyone else had noticed.

Marona and Junaray were released and were hugging their children like they would never let go. At last, we sat down to eat and relax a little. Everyone was slightly giddy but the atmosphere changed when Marcus cautioned us. "We still need to rendezvous with the Star Struck. And we need to make sure no one follows us. Then we need to make it to your planet. Joneb, we need to talk."

I followed him into a small room and sat down facing him. "Boy, you do get yourself in some fine messes. I thought you knew enough to stay away from the Planetary Alliance."

"I had no idea what was going on," I said defensively. Thinking back on the events, I still didn't know how I had landed in the middle of things again. Sometimes it just seemed like things followed me around.

"I know," Marcus growled. "certainly, didn't expect you to pop up there. Last time I heard, you had headed in the other direction." "And I noticed you have fallen for that girl. Oh, don't try to deny it."

"Now, what can you tell me about David? I want him to cooperate with us to discredit the Planetary alliance."

"I'm not sure what to say. I've only been with the Star Struck a couple of months. He's quiet but not unusually so. Doesn't talk much, always willing to help out."

"Hmm, sounds like the perfect plant—helpful but not annoying. I'll have to sound him out."

"How long till we join up with Star Struck?" I asked.

"About 24 hours" Marcus replied. "Go get some rest." Looking around the ship, I realized we had stretched the living quarters quite a bit. The women were all in the same room as Mamaroy and there was only one other crew room which was full. I settled down in a chair and got as comfortable as possible. I drifted off to sleep shortly. I was used to catching sleep wherever and whenever possible.

Chapter 8
THE RENDEZVOUS

I JERKED AWAKE, AWARE THAT THE ship had slowed down and an alarm was sounding. Instantly alert, I saw David sneaking toward the forward cabin. Following him, I saw him raise his hand with a wrench ready to strike the pilot. I yelled stop at the same time Marcus came out of the shadows and tackled him. "Everyone okay?"

Marcus looked around. Reassured, he looked down at David. "He wouldn't talk. I had hoped to get more information, but he didn't say a word, just sat there glaring at me. Secure him in the brig."

Taking the com link, he sent a series of sentences which sounded like a poem. Quite surprised, we all jumped when a reply came back after a short time. This was the code he had sent with Gilroy for Milroy. They were here and ready for boarding. A couple more phrases were exchanged and I was sent to round up the group.

Once again, our friendly giant scooped up

Mamaroy. "One more time," he murmured as he headed for the airlock passage. We were all encouraged to see her tentatively holding onto his neck. We hurried through the link into the Star Struck filled with a sense of urgency.

"Reunions later" Milroy commanded, his glance at Junaray filled with longing but he swung about. "Gilroy, take care of Mamaroy. The rest of you, emergency stations."

"Cast off the link."

"Casting off, clear"

"We have 10 minutes clearance before they come back," Gilroy sent this news to Marcus.

"Take off like you were told" was his reply. "We have your back."

We headed off in the opposite direction for a while, then went into an asteroid field. After a couple of hours, we headed in another direction entirely. Finally, we turned towards Argyle, their home planet.

Coming into land, we saw a group waiting

for us. Everyone was quiet as we surveyed the "welcoming party". They were well armed. "it's the Mackelrays," Milroy exclaimed. "I'll talk to them."

He stepped to the door, "Willison---".

"We heard you had been having problems. We're here to help."

Everyone on board was stunned. "Captain," I said, we need to get everyone off and into a safe place now".

"Right" he said. "Let's get moving."

Suddenly, there was an explosion in the sky. Everyone dived for cover as a ship plummeted down. It landed in a nearby field and the Mackelrays raced over. "We've got them", they yelled as survivors stumbled out of the wreckage. Things were a bit chaotic for a while, but eventually the crisis was sorted out.

Marcus and his men had tracked a Planetary Alliance ship to Argyle. Realizing they were going to attack Argyle, they fired on the enemy ship causing it to crash.

Mamaroy and Fitzroy were reunited in the

hospital and are recovering nicely. Junaray and Marona are back in their homes, dealing with their feelings, gradually settling in. Although things are strange right now, they are strong women and will soon feel safe and secure again.

Has Rojas forgiven me? I am about to find out. We have a rendezvous at that wonderful spot in 2 minutes. I have been here for an hour, waiting and worrying, hoping against hope. I hear a light footstep and look up. There she is looking even more beautiful.

I look at her, "I missed you so much" I started to say.

"Hush," she says. "I have missed you also. Forgive me" she looks down at the ground.

I reach her and taking her face in my hand, I tilt it up towards mine. Gently, I pull her close. "There is nothing to forgive".

Our lips touch, suddenly there are no more doubts. We kiss, holding on to each other, completely absorbed by joy and love, we stay locked in embrace as the sun goes down on Argyle.

Printed in the United States
By Bookmasters